Wilma and Biff saw a notice. It was about a go-kart race. Wilma had an idea. She told Biff about it.

Biff and Wilma were excited. They told Mum about the race.

"We need a go-kart," said Biff. "What about the old one?"

Mum went to the shed. She found the
old go-kart, but it was broken and rusty.
"Oh no!" said Biff.

Biff told Dad about the race. Dad
looked at the old go-kart.

"This one is broken," he said. "But we
can make a new one."

The mums and dads made a new go-kart. Everyone wanted to help. Biff and Mum looked at the plans. Wilma helped her dad.

Mum painted the go-kart. Chip helped.
He was good at painting.
"It looks brilliant!" said Biff.

Everyone looked at the new go-kart. Biff
wanted a go, but Mum said she couldn't.
The paint was still wet.

Mum took the children to a park. There
was a hill in the park. It was a good place
to try the new go-kart.

Wilma went first, but everyone had a go.
Biff went last.

"It's brilliant!" she said.

Wilma saw another go-kart.

"It's Anneena," she said. "She's got a go-kart too."

Everyone looked at Anneena's go-kart.

"It looks fast," said Wilma. "But I bet ours is faster."

"I bet it's not," said Anneena.

Wilma and Anneena had a race. The
go-karts raced down the hill. Anneena was
in front.

"Come on!" shouted Biff.

Suddenly, a dog ran in front of
Anneena. Her go-kart crashed into a bush.
Wilma crashed into Anneena.

Everyone looked at the go-karts.
Wilma's front wheels were bent. Anneena's
go-kart was broken. Everyone was upset.

Chip looked at the broken go-karts. He had an idea. He told Mum what the idea was.

"What a brilliant idea!" said Mum.

The mums and dads made a new
go-kart. They made one go-kart out of
two. They put the front of Anneena's go-
kart on the back of Wilma's.

The children liked the new go-kart. They called it Silver Bullet.

"What about the race?" asked Biff. "I bet Silver Bullet will win."

It was the day of the race. Everyone was excited.

"Look at all the go-karts!" said Biff.

Biff wanted to drive, but so did Wilma and Anneena. In the end, Mum tossed a coin and Anneena won.

It was time for the race.

"One ... two ... three ... go!" called the
starter.

"Come on, Anneena!" called Biff.

The go-karts raced down the hill.
Everyone shouted and cheered. Anneena
went fast. Silver Bullet was in front.

Anneena didn't win. Two go-karts went faster. Silver Bullet came third.

"Oh no!" said Biff.

Anneena was upset.

"I wanted to win," she said.

"Don't worry," said Biff. "Silver Bullet's still the best."

Silver Bullet did win a prize. It was the
best-looking go-kart.

"Hooray!" everyone cheered. "We said it
was the best!"